Santa Claus
Doesn't Mop
Floors

Santa Claus Doesn't Mop Floors

by
Debbie Dadey and Marcia Thornton Jones

illustrated by John Steven Gurney

A
LITTLE APPLE
PAPERBACK

SCHOLASTIC INC.

New York Toronto London Auckland Sydney

ISBN 0-590-44477-8

APPLE PAPERBACKS is a registered trademark of Scholastic Inc.

22 21 20 19 18   8 9/9 0 1 2/0

Printed in the U.S.A.   40

First Scholastic printing, October 1991

*To Allison, Jared, and Nathan —
and to Santa Claus!*

Contents

1

A Sticky Situation

"That's it!" Mr. Dobson, the janitor, screamed at the third-grade classroom. "I've had enough of your shenanigans."

Mrs. Ewing stared at Mr. Dobson from her desk. It was obvious she wasn't used to having an hysterical janitor at her door. She had only been the third-grade substitute teacher for one week, and she was already showing signs of battle fatigue. "Calm down, Mr. Dobson," she said. "Tell me what's wrong."

"I'll tell you what's wrong," he snapped. "Somebody took peanut butter from the food drive box and spread it all over the stair railing!" He held out his hands as proof. Sure enough, they were covered with brown sticky peanut butter.

1

"It looks like he's been making mud pies," Eddie giggled.

Mr. Dobson silenced him with a glare. "It was somebody in this class, wasn't it?"

Mrs. Ewing stood up. "Mr. Dobson, I'm sorry about the peanut butter, but I don't think you can blame anybody without proof."

Mr. Dobson looked like he was ready to explode. There wasn't a sound from

2

the kids as he hissed, "I have cleaned up vomit. I've mopped up sour milk from the floor. I have even scraped bubble gum from the ceilings in the bathroom. But this time it has gone too far. I will not clean up another mess made by these brats. I quit!"

"But you can't," Mrs. Ewing interrupted. "Christmas will be here in just a few weeks. How will you buy presents? Who will help clean up after the holiday parties?"

Mr. Dobson smiled like a lunatic. "My present will be to see these urchins clean up after themselves. And they can start with the stairs!" With that, he left.

Mrs. Ewing faced the third-grade class. Her red-painted lips were pressed in a thin line and a wrinkle messed up her forehead. She ran her fingers through her short curly hair and took a deep breath. "I can't believe anyone in this class would be so thoughtless, so cruel!" she said. "Mr. Dobson has worked hard to keep this building clean, and you repay him with a prank like that!"

Melody raised her hand. "But maybe it wasn't anyone in our class."

"Maybe not," Mrs. Ewing sighed. "I'd hate to think anyone in this room would take the food we've been collecting for the poor. But you do have a reputation for causing trouble."

Nobody could argue with her about that. They hadn't had recess for a month before Halloween. That's when each kid had brought in a spider to set loose in the principal's office. And then their teacher quit after she found her desk drawers full of shaving cream. Of course, everything changed after their new teacher, Mrs. Jeepers, came.

There was something about Mrs. Jeepers that made them straighten up fast.

Her eyes would flash at the first sign of trouble, and the green brooch she always wore would start to glow. Some kids thought she was some kind of monster or vampire. Before Mrs. Jeepers left for a Christmas vacation in Romania, she made the children promise to be nice to the substitute teacher. Unfortunately, Mrs. Jeepers forgot about Mr. Dobson.

Howie spoke up. "Mr. Dobson isn't really going to quit, is he? After all, he's threatened to leave before!"

Mrs. Ewing shook her head. "This time, I think he's serious."

"But who will clean the building?" Eddie asked.

Principal Davis interrupted from the door. "You will clean the building," he snapped. "Mr. Dobson has just quit his job, thanks to you."

Eddie sat up straight. "You can't prove it was us!"

"Oh, no?" Principal Davis stomped over to the trash can. Every kid in the room held his or her breath as the principal stooped down and pulled out two empty peanut butter jars. "How do you explain these?"

Eddie jabbed Howie in the back. "You moron," he sputtered. "You should have dumped those in another class!"

But it was too late now.

"Until I find a replacement for Mr. Dobson," Principal Davis said through clenched teeth, "this class is in charge of cleaning. And you can start with the stair railing!"

2

Mr. Jolly

"I wonder when Principal Davis is going to hire a new janitor?" Liza asked as she pushed blonde hair out of her eyes.

Eddie slapped the mop around on the hall floor. "It's been a whole week since Mr. Dobson quit. I'm sick of emptying trash and mopping the floors every recess."

"We wouldn't be doing it at all if you hadn't come up with that peanut butter idea," Howie snapped.

"It was only peanut butter!" Eddie sputtered.

Melody tugged on her black braid. "It really wasn't a nice thing to do. And now poor Mr. Dobson is without a job during Christmas!"

"It was his choice!" Eddie's face was

turning as red as his hair. "He didn't have to quit. Besides, who cares about Christmas anyway!"

Liza, Howie, and Melody looked at each other. Ever since Eddie's mother had died, his father refused to celebrate Christmas.

"Everybody likes Christmas," Liza said softly.

"Not me!" Eddie announced. "Christmas is for sissies."

"Sissies!" boomed a deep voice behind them.

All four kids turned to see Principal Davis and a very fat man standing in the hall.

"I'd like to introduce Mr. Jolly," Principal Davis said. "He's our new janitor."

Mr. Jolly smiled at them. His blue eyes twinkled under his bushy white eyebrows, and a smile could barely be seen from under his thick white beard and

mustache. A thin curl of smoke circled above the pipe he puffed on. He could've passed for somebody's grandfather if it hadn't been for his clothes. Most grandfathers don't wear hot pink T-shirts with green-and-pink slacks. He even had on bright green tennis shoes to match.

Melody broke the silence. "We sure are glad to meet you."

"I bet you are," Mr. Jolly chuckled as he took the mop from Eddie. "Now you kids can go out to recess, and I'll clean up this mess," he said as he pulled his beard. And with that he began mopping the floor. The keys hanging from his green belt jingled as he worked. The floor seemed to sparkle wherever he mopped.

"Boy, he sure works fast," Liza commented.

"Who cares?" Eddie said. "Let's get outside."

Once they were on the playground, the four ex-janitors gathered under the oak tree. Their breaths looked like Mr. Jolly's pipe smoke as they talked.

"Mr. Jolly sure seems nice," Liza said.

"But he's awfully fat," Howie pointed out.

Melody rolled her eyes. "Big deal, so he's fat. I'm just glad we don't have to mop the floor anymore."

Howie wanted to be a doctor, and he was always talking about health. "Being fat is bad for you."

"So's this, ice breath," Eddie said with a laugh. And then he smacked Howie right in the face with a snowball.

After that, it was all-out war. The four kids were so busy throwing snowballs, they didn't see that Mr. Jolly was watching them from the window, and that he was writing things down in a little red notebook.

3

A Peculiar Helper

Nobody gave Mr. Jolly a second thought. At least, not until the end of that week. They were all sitting at the lunch table, slurping down chicken noodle soup.

"Who is that?" Melody asked with wide eyes.

Howie, Eddie, and Liza glanced across the room.

"It's Mr. Jolly," Liza said, as if she had just solved a hard math problem.

"I know that," Melody snapped. "But who's that with him?"

"I don't see anybody," Howie said.

Eddie shook his head. "I think Melody has gone nuts!"

"I have not," Melody hissed. "You just can't see him."

"I told you she's gone bananas," Eddie

said confidently. "Now she's even seeing things."

Melody slammed her spoon on the table. "I'm perfectly fine. You just can't see him because he's behind Mr. Jolly. Look over there now."

They all looked as a very short man walked around Mr. Jolly. He looked just like any school kid, except for his pointy black beard. He was dressed in green from head to toe, and he even wore a little green hat. He waved his arms like he was excited. Mr. Jolly nodded his head every once in a while.

"I've never seen anybody so short," Liza whispered.

"He can't help it if he's short," Howie said smugly.

"I want to know what they're talking about," Eddie said as he stood up. "Let's go find out."

Howie grabbed Eddie. "That's eaves-
dropping."

"So?" Eddie shrugged.

"Listening to other people talking isn't
very nice," Melody chimed in.

"Who said I'm nice?" Eddie said as he
pulled away from Howie. "You'll come,
too, if you want to find out who the little
man is!"

Liza, Howie, and Melody looked at each
other and then followed Eddie. They carried their trays to the trash cans the long
way around the cafeteria so they'd have
to walk right behind Mr. Jolly and the
little man.

"It's a mess, S.C.," the little man was
saying. "You'll have to come straighten
it out. It's too close to Christmas for you
to be fooling around as a janitor. There's
real work to be done!"

Mr. Jolly interrupted him. "Eli, this is

real work. There's not a thing wrong with being a janitor."

"But we need you at home!"

"You can manage by yourselves, Eli," Mr. Jolly said. "I've got work to do here."

Suddenly Eli cleared his throat and pointed to the four kids with their trays. Howie, Eddie, and Melody looked away as they walked behind Mr. Jolly. But Liza froze.

"We weren't listening," Liza said too loudly. "We were just putting our trays away."

Mr. Jolly tugged on his beard and looked down at her. "You took the long way around, didn't you?" he asked.

Liza looked like she was ready to faint. Instead she barely nodded.

"Well," Mr. Jolly chuckled, "you better go put your tray away, then."

Mr. Jolly glanced down at his friend, Eli. "Like I said, I've got work to do here." Then he pulled out his notebook and began to write in it.

4

A Chill in the Air

"It's freezing in here," Eddie complained. It was the morning after Eli had been in the cafeteria. Eddie, Melody, Liza, and Howie were the first children in their classroom.

"You can see your breath, it's so cold," Howie said. They all took turns blowing cold smoke rings at each other.

"I bet that new janitor forgot to turn on the heat," Liza said.

"What's he trying to do, freeze us to death?" Melody shivered and hugged herself to keep warm.

"We better go find him and tell him to turn up the thermostat," Howie suggested. "Before Principal Davis gets mad and fires him!"

The four kids went to the janitor's room

in the basement. Sure enough, there was Mr. Jolly, filling a bucket with sudsy water.

Melody grabbed Howie. "He must be crazy! He's wearing shorts!"

"And a T-shirt," Howie whispered.

The sight of Mr. Jolly's bare legs and arms made Liza shiver. The new janitor still wore his bright green tennis shoes — and no socks!

"Well, good morning," he boomed when he saw the four children. "What can I do for you?"

"We thought we'd remind you to turn on the heat," Howie said. "It's a bit cold here this morning." Little clouds formed as Howie spoke, to prove his point.

"Nonsense!" Mr. Jolly laughed. "It was way too warm in here. I finally had to turn the heat down so I wouldn't melt."

"But it's the dead of winter," Eddie interrupted.

"It's freezing outside," Melody added.

Mr. Jolly peeped out the little window. "Why, there isn't even the tiniest snowflake out there, not a glimmer of ice, nor a spot of slush. It's practically summer today! Now, you kids scoot to class!" With that, Mr. Jolly continued mixing white bubbles into his bucket.

Eddie led his friends down the hall. "I thought this guy was weird," he said. "He's short on brains, as well as having short friends!"

Liza pulled her jacket tight. "I guess we'll just have to make do."

"Not me!" Eddie exclaimed. "I'm getting some heat."

Eddie turned and stomped away, with his friends following. He turned a corner and opened a closet.

"What are you doing?" Howie whispered. "We're not allowed in there."

"We're not allowed to do much of anything," Eddie said as he turned on a light. "But that's never stopped me before." Then he pointed to a big thermostat on the wall. "That's just what we need." Eddie twisted the dial.

"Our worries are over," he said as he shut the closet door. "It ought to be warming up in no time flat."

Eddie was right. In less than twenty minutes they were able to shed their

coats. Some kids even took off their sweaters. They were just settling down to their English work when Melody decided she had to go to the bathroom.

Eddie watched as she left the room, then he raised his hand.

"Yes, Eddie?" Mrs. Ewing asked.

"I need to get something out in the hall," Eddie said. "I need my pencil."

"Well . . . make it quick," Mrs. Ewing snapped.

"Sure thing," Eddie said as he rushed out the door. He spied Melody at the water fountain. She was leaning over, slurping loudly. Eddie sneaked up behind her and dunked her head into the ice-cold water.

Melody stood up, sputtering. "I'm going to get you for that," she said, curling her hand into a fist.

But before she had a chance to

sock him a really good one, Mr. Jolly walked around the corner and ran right into Eddie.

"Gee, Mr. Jolly," Eddie snapped. "You ought to watch where you're going!"

"It serves you right," Melody giggled. Then she glanced up at Mr. Jolly. "Are you okay?"

Mr. Jolly pulled on his beard. A little river of sweat trickled down his nose and then dripped to the floor. He pulled out a green-and-white-checked handkerchief and wiped off his face. "Yes, I think I'll be just fine," he said. "It's just that it's so warm in this blasted building. I can't stand warm temperatures."

"It feels fine to me," Melody said.

"Yeah," Eddie huffed. "It's much warmer than this morning."

Mr. Jolly looked thoughtfully at Eddie, and then he pulled out his little red notebook and jotted something down.

"You're always writing stuff down," Eddie commented. "What is that notebook for, anyway?"

Mr. Jolly dabbed at his forehead. "Oh, it's just a list of some things. But I don't have time to talk now. I have to do something about this temperature." And with a jingling of keys, he was gone.

"Did you hear that?" Eddie groaned. "He'll see that we turned up the thermostat."

But there was nothing Eddie and Melody could do about it because Mrs. Ewing rushed out into the hall and took them each by the arm. "Into the classroom and to your work," she snapped. "This instant!"

They hadn't even finished their English when the temperature started to drop. Mrs. Ewing was the first to notice. She shivered and slipped into her sweater. It wasn't long before all the kids in the class had their sweaters on, too.

Liza rubbed her hands together. "It's so cold, I can hardly write," she whispered.

Howie nodded as he stuck his hands under his armpits. "My hands feel like a frozen fish," he moaned.

During math, Melody started to sniff. "My nose is starting to run."

"I think my pencil is frozen to my hand," Eddie groaned.

By recess time, the kids in Mrs. Ewing's third grade were so cold they didn't even want to go outside. "Nonsense," Mrs. Ewing scolded. "Some fresh air is just what we need. Maybe if we all get some exercise, we'll warm up."

All the kids buttoned up their coats and put on their mittens as they filed outside.

"I don't believe it!" Howie yelled. "It's warmer outside than inside!"

It was true. With the sun shining on them, it felt ten degrees warmer.

"Mr. Jolly's gonna freeze us to death this winter," Melody said. "He told us he hates it warm."

"Maybe we could turn the thermostat back up," Liza suggested.

"No," Howie moaned. "Mr. Jolly would just turn it back to the arctic zone."

"Well, I'm not going to freeze to death all winter long," Eddie snapped.

"What can YOU do?" Melody asked.

Eddie smiled. "I'll make him sorry he ever heard of Bailey Elementary School. He'll be so tired from cleaning up after me, he won't have time to mess with the temperature."

"You can't do that," Liza insisted.

"Why not?" Eddie asked.

"If you do, he'll probably quit his job. And it's almost Christmas. What would Mr. Jolly do without a job during the holidays?" Liza asked.

"Christmas is nothing but a scheme by stores to make suckers spend money. He'll be better off without a job!" Eddie said.

"But Principal Davis would kill us," Melody reminded him.

"I'm not afraid of him," Eddie said. "I'm not afraid of anyone."

5

A Jolly Disaster

By lunchtime, Eddie had already figured out a plan.

"I know how to get rid of Mr. Jolly," he announced at the lunch table.

"What are you going to do?" Howie asked.

"It's what WE'RE going to do," Eddie said. "I want you all to help me."

"I don't know," Howie said as he stuffed his mouth with a pickle. "Principal Davis caught us the last time I let you talk me into one of your dumb tricks."

"That was your own fault for putting the peanut butter jars in our trash can," Eddie said.

"I don't care," Howie said firmly. "I'm not helping this time."

"Me, neither," added Liza and Melody.

"Fine," Eddie snapped. "I don't need your help anyway. I'll do it myself."

When they were back in their classroom, Eddie raised his hand. "Mrs. Ewing, may I go to the bathroom?" he asked in a sickly sweet voice.

"I suppose," Mrs. Ewing said. "But hurry. We're getting ready to start the science lesson."

Eddie nodded seriously as he left the room.

Once he was in the hall Eddie acted fast. He dashed into the boys' bathroom and stuffed every roll of toilet paper under his shirt. "I look like a lumpy Santa," he laughed when he saw himself in the mirror.

Then he slipped back into the hall and started walking. I have to find the perfect place, he said to himself. Where they'd never suspect I'd been.

He peeked into the girls' bathroom but then shook his head. Too risky, he thought. A girl could walk in any minute.

He glanced at the clock hanging on the wall. It was halfway between lunch and the end of school. Every class in the building was busy trying to finish their day's work.

That's when it hit him. The perfect idea. He turned a corner and headed straight for the teachers' lounge.

Once inside he dumped his load of toilet paper and started to drape it over every piece of furniture. He stuffed wads inside the ditto machine and coffee maker. He even hung some from the lights by standing on a chair.

When he was finished, he looked at his work. "Perfect," he said. "This mess

ought to keep any janitor busy."

Before running back to his classroom, Eddie made a quick detour to the basement closet.

Mrs. Ewing was saying some stuff about solids and liquids when Eddie sailed into the room.

Eddie sat down and winked at Howie. "I turned the heat up, and that stupid janitor won't be turning it down anytime soon!" Eddie whispered.

"Why's that?" Howie whispered back.

"It'll take him three days just to clean up the mess I made in the teachers' room." Eddie couldn't help feeling proud of himself. And he was already feeling warmer.

"Eddie, did you want to say something to the class?" Mrs. Ewing interrupted.

"No, thanks," Eddie said loudly.

"Please pay attention to the lesson, then," Mrs. Ewing said as she began writing on the board.

"I've gotta see this," Howie whispered. Mrs. Ewing wasn't very happy when Howie asked to go to the bathroom, but she let him go anyway.

Howie was only gone a few minutes. He came back in the room shaking his head. "You liar," he whispered to Eddie. "There's no mess in the teachers' lounge. It's as clean as a whistle!"

"What?" Eddie tried to whisper. "I put toilet paper everywhere. There's no way Mr. Jolly could've cleaned it up that fast."

"There's nothing there now," Howie shrugged. "Nothing but Mr. Jolly."

"That can't be!" Eddie shivered. Was it his imagination, or was it already getting colder?

6

Checking It Twice

As soon as Mrs. Ewing dismissed them that afternoon, Eddie grabbed his friends in the hall.

"We've got to go to the teachers' lounge," Eddie said. "Something strange is happening."

"Oh, Eddie," Howie sighed. "Why don't you just admit you lied? You didn't do anything to the teachers' lounge."

"But I did," Eddie yelled. "And I'm going to find out who undid it!" Eddie turned and stomped toward the lounge.

Melody, Liza, and Howie looked at each other and then followed.

The lounge was full of teachers, drinking coffee as they tried to stay warm. But the four kids were able to peek inside long enough to see a sparkling clean room.

"Isn't that Mr. Jolly great?" they heard Mrs. Ewing say. "I just wish he wouldn't keep the building so cold."

"But this place has never been so clean," another teacher agreed. "I don't know how he does it!"

"It's almost like magic!" Mrs. Ewing said. "Speaking of magic, did you hear about the food drive? The box was over-

flowing with jars of peanut butter, and no one will admit to bringing them in!"

Eddie pulled away from the door. "Magic, my eyeball. That Mr. Jolly is nothing but a cold-blooded old geezer."

"Watch out," Melody warned Eddie. "He's standing right behind you."

Sure enough, Mr. Jolly had listened to every word they said. And he was writing in his little red notebook.

"Hello, boys and girls." Mr. Jolly smiled as he slipped his red notebook into a pocket. "I thought you kids would stay far away from the teachers' lounge!"

"Oh, we just had to show Eddie how clean it was," Liza blurted.

Eddie jabbed her in the ribs. "The lounge *is* awfully clean," Eddie muttered.

Mr. Jolly winked. "Let's keep it that way, too."

"It's not up to us to keep it clean," Eddie said.

Mr. Jolly rubbed his beard. "And it's not up to you to make the messes."

"Let's get out of here," Eddie said.

" 'Bye Mr. Jolly," Liza and Howie waved.

The four kids ran outside and met under the big oak tree.

"There's something weird about Mr. Jolly," Eddie announced.

"It is creepy the way he watches us," Melody agreed.

"And why is he always writing in that notebook?" Liza asked.

"It's like he's writing down everything we do," Howie added.

"Maybe he's a spy," Eddie teased.

Melody rolled her eyes. "Why would anyone want to spy on us?"

"He could be Santa Claus," Liza suggested quietly.

Eddie burst out laughing. "Liza, why don't you grow up?"

"Wait a minute," Howie interrupted. "Mr. Jolly does keep the building as cold as the North Pole."

"And what about the little man all dressed in green?" Melody added. "He could've been one of Santa's elves!"

"Didn't that little guy call him S.C.?" Liza asked. "That could be short for Santa Claus."

"You guys act like you're in kindergarten," Eddie sneered. "Santa Claus is kids' stuff!"

"Maybe you're right," Melody said. "After all, Santa Claus doesn't mop floors. And I've never seen Santa wearing shorts or green tennis shoes."

"How would you know?" Liza asked. "Maybe he's just pretending to be a janitor."

"Mr. Jolly is just an old man who's trying to turn us into Freeze Pops," Eddie said. "But I'm not going to let him!"

7

Let It Snow!

Eddie waited under the big oak tree the next morning. A few snowflakes whirled to the ground as Melody walked up. The grass was so cold it scrunched under her feet.

"I've got the perfect plan," Eddie said quickly.

"Plan for what?" Melody asked.

"A surefire plan to make Mr. Jolly Janitor forget all about turning down the heat," Eddie said firmly.

"He does keep the building awfully cold," Melody nodded.

"Then you'll help me?" Eddie asked.

"I don't know," Melody said. "What're you going to do?"

"Come on, I'll show you," Eddie said, and motioned for his friend to follow as he started walking toward the school.

"Why don't we wait for Liza and Howie?" Melody suggested.

"We have to act fast, before Mr. Jolly and everybody comes. Are you coming or not?"

Melody shivered. "I guess," she said reluctantly. She followed Eddie into the hallway and watched as he pulled five huge cans of whipped cream from his bookbag.

"What are you going to do with those?" Melody asked.

"Mr. Jolly likes it cold, right?" Eddie asked.

"Right," Melody agreed.

"We're going to give Mr. Jolly what he wants. We're going to make it snow in the halls!" Eddie grabbed a can in each hand and started squirting the walls.

"I don't think this is a good idea," Melody said as she watched.

"Don't be such a chicken," Eddie teased, "and start helping!"

"I'm no chicken," Melody snapped. She grabbed a can and wrote Mr. Jolly's name on the wall.

Eddie put one can down, squirted a mountain of whipped cream in his hand, and then slurped it up. "Hey! This makes a great breakfast."

Melody squirted a stream straight into her mouth. "Mmmmm, this is good," she said.

They took turns squirting heaps of snow-white whipped cream on the wall and then in their mouths. By the time they finished, the hall looked like it had been hit by a blizzard.

"This will keep Mr. Jolly so busy, he won't have time to think about the temperature," Eddie said.

"You're right," Melody agreed.

Eddie quickly threw all the empty cans into the second grade's trash can.

"Let's get out of here," Melody whispered. "I think I hear someone coming."

They both heard Mr. Jolly's keys jingling not too far away.

Eddie nodded. "Let's go turn up the heat. This mess is gonna keep Mr. Jolly busy all morning long."

Melody giggled. "I'm afraid he won't be so jolly when he sees this!"

Liza was just getting a drink from the water fountain when Melody and Eddie rushed to their classroom. Eddie went straight into the room, but Melody whispered to Liza about the whipped cream.

"I can't believe you'd do something so awful," Liza cried.

"It was only whipped cream," Melody said uneasily. "It's not like it was paint."

"Eddie is always doing something rotten," Liza said, wiping water off her mouth. "But I thought you were nice."

"I am nice," Melody snapped.

"I bet Mr. Jolly doesn't think so," Liza said.

"He doesn't know I did it," Melody said, slurping down a big gulp of water.

"What if he is Santa Claus?" Liza asked. "Santa Claus sees everything. Just like the song says, 'He sees you when you're sleeping, he knows — ' "

"Mr. Jolly isn't Santa Claus," Melody insisted.

"Maybe not," Liza agreed. "But what if he is? Are you willing to take that chance?"

Melody shrugged her shoulders. "Oh, all right. I guess I could help clean up some of the mess."

"I'll help, too," Liza offered.

"You're really a good friend," Melody

said gratefully as they headed down the hallway.

Liza stopped in her tracks when she rounded the corner. "I thought this was where you put the whipped cream."

"It was," Melody said.

"There's nothing there now," Liza pointed.

Melody stared in disbelief. The wall was sparkling clean. Not one trace of whipped cream was anywhere to be seen.

"I don't get it," Melody said. "We used enough whipped cream to cover Wyoming. It would've taken Mr. Jolly all day to clean it up."

"Unless . . ." Liza said.

"Unless what?" Melody asked.

"Unless he really is Santa Claus," Liza whispered.

8

Magic?

"Eddie, I've got to tell you something," Melody whispered when she went into the room.

"Leave me alone," Eddie grumbled. "I don't feel very good."

"But I've got to tell you about Mr. Jolly," Melody insisted. "He's magic."

"What are you talking about?" Eddie said. His face looked greener than the

Christmas paper chains that decorated the room.

"Mr. Jolly cleaned up the whipped cream mess already," Melody whispered.

"Nobody could've cleaned it up that fast," Eddie muttered.

"Nobody but Santa," Melody whispered.

"Mr. Jolly may be fast, but he sure isn't Santa Claus. Even if there was a Santa Claus, he sure wouldn't be a big fat janitor." Eddie groaned and laid his head down.

"Maybe every year Santa Claus goes to a different school and gets to know the children there . . . ," Melody wondered out loud.

"Yeah," Eddie squeaked, "and maybe the Easter Bunny is the old lady that burns the hamburgers in the cafeteria."

"Eddie, I'm serious," Melody said.

"I'm serious, too," Eddie groaned. "I

ate too much whipped cream. I think I'm gonna be sick." Eddie ran up to the front of the room. Mrs. Ewing took one look at his face and sent him to the office.

"I'm sick," Eddie moaned when he got there.

"Too much whipped cream will make anyone sick," Mr. Jolly laughed from one side of the office. He was busy writing in his little red notebook.

"I haven't been eating any whipped cream," Eddie lied. "I think I may have the flu. I need to go home."

"I'll call your dad right away," the secretary told Eddie.

Eddie walked over to Mr. Jolly and tried to peek in his book. But Mr. Jolly snapped it shut and put it in his shorts pocket.

"What are you always writing about in that little red notebook?" Eddie asked.

"Oh, I like to notice things about people and write them down," Mr. Jolly said.

"In other words," Eddie said, "you're spying."

"I wouldn't exactly call it spying," Mr. Jolly said, smiling. "I just call it observing."

"Did you observe something about me?" Eddie asked.

"As a matter of fact, I did," Mr. Jolly said. "I noticed that you don't believe in Christmas or Santa Claus."

"Christmas is for little kids, and even if there was a Santa Claus, he couldn't bring me what I want for Christmas," Eddie said as he rubbed his aching stomach.

"And what is it you want — ?" Mr. Jolly started to ask. But before he finished, Eddie couldn't hold the whipped cream anymore. Out it came, along with most of Eddie's breakfast, all over Mr. Jolly's feet.

Mr. Jolly's big ring of keys jingled as

the secretary rushed Eddie to the bath-room.

In a few minutes, Eddie and the secretary came back into the office. Eddie looked like a sick walrus as he slumped into a chair.

The secretary didn't look too great, either. She glanced at Mr. Jolly's clean tennis shoes. "Didn't he . . . ?" She pointed. "Weren't those covered with . . . ?" The secretary shook her head. "Oh, never mind, I have to get in touch with Eddie's father."

"You can just forget about that," Eddie snapped. "He's not home and he won't be home until after Christmas."

"There has to be someone we can call," the secretary said.

"Maybe my grandmother will come get me," Eddie moaned. "If she isn't too busy."

Mr. Jolly sat down next to Eddie while

the secretary started dialing. "I'm sure your grandmother will come for you," Mr. Jolly said. "And when she does, you be sure to tell her you got sick on whipped cream."

"I told you I haven't eaten any whipped cream," Eddie insisted meekly.

Mr. Jolly chuckled as he stood up to leave. "I'm going to turn that heat down. And by the way, whipped cream doesn't look a thing like snow."

9

Ho! Ho! Ho!

"Don't you think it's weird?" Melody asked Eddie the next morning.

"What?" Eddie asked.

"That Mr. Jolly knew you wanted the whipped cream to look like snow?" Howie said.

"I'll tell you something else that's weird," Liza said. "The food drive box was filled with cans of whipped cream!"

They were all gathered around the water fountain the next morning. Eddie wasn't green anymore.

"I'm telling you," Liza insisted, "he's Santa Claus."

"She may be right," Melody agreed. "After all, have you ever heard of anybody named Jolly before?"

"And his initials are S.C.," Howie added.

Eddie kicked the wall. "S.C. probably just stands for sour cabbage," he grumbled. "I won't believe he's Santa Claus until I see him fly through the sky in his sleigh."

"Maybe we better be careful, just in case," Liza suggested.

"In case he really is Santa," Howie agreed.

"I do want lots of presents for Christmas," Melody added.

"You guys have slush for brains," Eddie interrupted. "I know Mr. Jolly isn't Santa Claus, and I'm going to prove it."

"How?" they all asked together.

"I'm going to follow him home after school," Eddie said.

"What will that prove?" Howie asked.

"When you see the dump Mr. Jolly lives in, it'll prove he's just an ordinary fat person. Anybody who's not a chicken will come with me!" Eddie dared.

That afternoon Eddie and Howie hid in the bathroom when the last bell rang.

"We've got to figure out a way to watch Mr. Jolly without him seeing us," Eddie said.

"That'll be impossible if he really is Santa Claus," Howie said.

Eddie rolled his eyes. "C'mon," he said, "let's wait in the oak tree until he leaves. Then we can follow him."

Howie grabbed Eddie's arm. "Don't we need to find Melody and Liza?"

"Naw," Eddie said, "they went home. I knew they'd be too chicken."

Howie and Eddie sneaked out of the building and into the freezing wind.

"Oh, it's colder than a penguin's nose out here," Eddie complained.

"We'll freeze if we stay here until Mr. Jolly gets finished. It'll take him a long time to clean the whole building," Howie whined.

"Do you want to find out the truth or not?" Eddie snapped.

"Not if it means turning into the Abominable Snowman," Howie said, shivering.

"Shut up and climb the tree," Eddie ordered.

The two boys sat on the icy branches and waited.

Howie's toes didn't have time to get cold. With a jingling of keys, Mr. Jolly came out of the building. He carried a big bag slung over his shoulders.

Howie elbowed Eddie in the ribs. "Look! He's carrying a bag of toys!"

Both boys watched as Mr. Jolly tossed the huge bag into the trash bin.

"No, frost face, it was only garbage," Eddie whispered.

Mr. Jolly took a deep breath and patted his bulging stomach. He lit his pipe and then jingled his keys again. As if by magic, a bright red sports car sped up.

The driver was so short he could barely see over the steering wheel. But the boys knew who it was as soon as they saw his green hat and pointy black beard. It was Eli.

Eli backed the shiny red car into the space in front of Mr. Jolly. That's when Howie noticed it. He jabbed Eddie and pointed. Even Eddie was speechless for once as he read the license plate. In green letters it said, "Ho! Ho! Ho!"

10

You Better Watch Out

"He really IS Santa Claus," Howie shrieked. Mr. Jolly and Eli turned to look at the oak tree.

"Shhh," Eddie hissed. "They'll hear you!" He reached across some branches to slap his hand over Howie's mouth. But Howie pulled back and Eddie ended up grabbing empty air.

"Ahhh!" Eddie screamed as he fell to the frozen ground.

Mr. Jolly and Eli came rushing over.

"Are you all right?" Mr. Jolly asked.

"I . . . I think so," Eddie stammered.

Eli helped Eddie to his feet. "There's another one up there, S.C.," he said as he pointed up to Howie.

Howie slithered down from the tree and

landed at Mr. Jolly's feet. "You are Santa Claus, aren't you?" Howie shouted.

Eli gasped, but Mr. Jolly just tugged at his beard. "Now, whatever gave you that idea?"

"I knew it!" Howie yelled. "See, Eddie, I told you so!"

Eddie stood up straight and stared hard at Mr. Jolly. "He never said he was. And even if he did, I wouldn't believe it!"

"What a rude little boy," Eli interrupted. "Really, S.C., I don't see why you put up with him."

Eddie turned to Eli. "I'd watch who you were calling *little*, mistletoe breath!"

Mr. Jolly put a hand on both of their shoulders. "Settle down, both of you."

Eli took a deep breath and let it out slowly. Howie could smell peppermint on his breath.

"I believe we should leave, S.C.," Eli

said quietly. "You've messed around with these kids long enough."

"You can't leave now, Santa!" Howie squeaked.

Mr. Jolly laughed, but not the way most grown-ups do. This laugh came from deep inside him. Then he puffed on his pipe, letting the smoke curl around his head. "Your friend doesn't seem to agree with you," he said as he nodded at Eddie.

"Eddie doesn't agree with anyone," Howie said. "But that doesn't mean anything!"

Eddie punched Howie on the arm. "I think you've got ice cubes for brains, and half of them are melted."

"See," Howie said. "He's just rotten."

Mr. Jolly shook his head. "Perhaps. Or perhaps he just needs Christmas spirit."

"Quit talking about me!" Eddie yelled. "You're nothing but a crazy fat man with a short friend. You're going to be sorry you ever saw Bailey Elementary School!" And then he stomped away.

11

Santa's Challenge

"Wait a minute," Howie yelled after Eddie. Howie had chased Eddie two blocks and was breathing hard when he finally caught up with him.

"What do you want?" Eddie screamed.

"Don't be mad at me," Howie squeaked. "I'm your friend."

"Some friend," Eddie grumbled. "Do you always go around telling people I'm rotten?"

"No," Howie said. "Please don't be mad, I've got to tell you something."

"What now?" Eddie asked.

"Santa, I mean Mr. Jolly, told me something." Howie's voice was almost in a whisper.

"What?" Eddie asked again.

Howie looked around to see if anyone

was listening. "He told me that we had our work cut out for us."

"What work?" Eddie asked impatiently.

"Making you believe in Christmas," Howie announced.

"I told you, Christmas is for little kids," Eddie snapped. "If my own father doesn't even care about Christmas, then why should I?"

"Because Christmas is a special time,"

Howie said softly. "Why, it's a time of believing in miracles. Isn't it a miracle that Santa Claus is at our school?"

"Miracles," Eddie sputtered. "I don't believe in miracles or Santa Claus. If Santa Claus can't make my father believe in Christmas, then there really isn't a Santa Claus and there sure aren't any miracles."

Howie shook his head sadly as Eddie stomped off. This time, Howie didn't follow him.

12

Santa's Miracle

"Brace yourself," Howie said as Eddie walked into the classroom the next morning. Mrs. Ewing was writing the assignments on the board.

Melody shook her head and whispered, "There's no telling what Eddie's going to do to poor Mr. Jolly today."

"You mean Santa Claus," Liza corrected.

"Eddie will blow his chances to ever celebrate Christmas if he does something terrible to Mr. Jolly, I mean Santa," Howie said.

They all got quiet as Eddie sat down. Eddie smiled but didn't say a word.

"Hi, Eddie," Howie said.

"Hi!" Eddie smiled back.

"Why are you so quiet this morning?" Melody asked.

"I can't tell you yet," Eddie said with a big smile on his face. "I have to see Mr. Jolly first."

Mrs. Ewing stopped writing on the board when she heard Eddie. "Children," she said, "I just found out that Mr. Jolly is gone. Principal Davis said Mr. Jolly called him late last night to tell him that he had to quit. It seems he found work up north."

"Oh, no!" Howie moaned. "Do we have to clean the building again?"

Mrs. Ewing smiled. "Luckily, Mr. Dobson has agreed to give us another try."

"Oh," Eddie said, "I wanted to tell Mr. Jolly something."

"What did you want to tell him?" Liza asked.

"I wanted to tell him thank you," Eddie said. "And I wanted to tell him I believe in miracles."

70

"What changed your mind?" Howie asked.

"My dad came home late last night. He's going to stay for Christmas." Eddie smiled broadly. "My dad said it was time we had Christmas joy at our house."

Creepy, weird, wacky and funny things happen to the Bailey School Kids!™ Collect and read them all!

The Adventures of THE BAILEY SCHOOL KIDS®